Disney
PRINCESS

12 Days of
Princess

Written by **Holly Rice**

Illustrated by **John John Bajet**

Disney PRESS
Los Angeles • New York

On the **first** day of Christmas,
a *princess* gave to me...

A red rose
in a bell jar.

On the second day of Christmas,
a princess gave to me...

Two glass slippers

And a red rose
in a bell jar.

On the **third** day of Christmas,
a *princess* gave to me...

Three good fairies,

Two glass slippers,

And a red rose
in a bell jar.

On the **fourth** day of Christmas,
a *princess* gave to **me** ...

Four bows and arrows,

Three good fairies,

Two glass slippers,

And a red rose
in a bell jar.

On the **fifth** day of Christmas,
a *princess* gave to **me** ...

Five jazz players,
Four bows and arrows,
Three good fairies,
Two glass slippers,

And a red rose
in a bell jar.

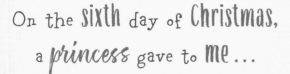

On the **sixth** day of Christmas,
a *princess* gave to me...

Six mermaids swimming,
Five jazz players,
Four bows and arrows,
Three good fairies,
Two glass slippers,

And a red rose
in a bell jar.

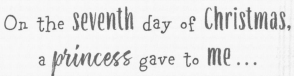

On the **seventh** day of Christmas,
a *princess* gave to **me**...

Seven dwarfs a-caroling,
Six mermaids swimming,
Five jazz players,
Four bows and arrows,
Three good fairies,
Two glass slippers,

And a red rose
in a bell jar.

On the **eighth** day of Christmas,
a *princess* gave to me...

Eight mice a-wrapping,

Seven dwarfs a-caroling,

Six mermaids swimming,

Five jazz players,

Four bows and arrows,

Three good fairies,

Two glass slippers,

And a red rose
in a bell jar.

On the **ninth** day of Christmas,
a *princess* gave to **me**...

Nine glowing lanterns,

Eight mice a-wrapping,

Seven dwarfs a-caroling,

Six mermaids swimming,

Five jazz players,

Four bows and arrows,

Three good fairies,

Two glass slippers,

And a red rose
in a bell jar.

On the **tenth** day of Christmas,
a *princess* gave to **me**...

Ten dinglehoppers,
Nine glowing lanterns,
Eight mice a-wrapping,
Seven dwarfs a-caroling,
Six mermaids swimming,
Five jazz players,
Four bows and arrows,
Three good fairies,
Two glass slippers,

And a red rose
in a bell jar.

On the **eleventh** day of Christmas,
a *princess* gave to me...

Eleven teacups dancing,
Ten dinglehoppers,
Nine glowing lanterns,
Eight mice a-wrapping,
Seven dwarfs a-caroling,
Six mermaids swimming,
Five jazz players,
Four bows and arrows,
Three good fairies,
Two glass slippers,

And a red rose
in a bell jar.

On the **twelfth** day of Christmas,
a *princess* gave to me...

Twelve
stars for wishing...

Eleven
teacups dancing,

Ten
dinglehoppers,

Nine
glowing lanterns,

Five
jazz players,

Four
bows and arrows,

Three
good fairies,

Eight

mice a-wrapping,

Seven

dwarfs a-caroling,

Six

mermaids swimming,

Two

glass slippers,

And a red rose in a bell jar.